ELLEN AND PENGUIN AND THE NEW BABY

CLARA VULLIAMY

WALKER BOOKS
AND SUBSIDIARIES
LONDON • BOSTON • SYDNEY

KU-092-908

Ellen had a new baby brother.

Penguin wasn't sure if he liked
new baby brothers much.

Everywhere Ellen and Penguin went,

the baby came too.

When they wanted a quiet story,
the baby started crying.

And because Mum
was too busy to
help them,

a lot went
wrong.

The baby was given Ellen's old mobile
with the woolly sheep hanging down.

"Penguin's cross," said Ellen.

"He likes that mobile."

Ellen and Penguin got into the baby's
carrycot and pretended it was a little boat
taking them far away to sea.

"You'd better get out
or you'll break it," said Mum.

In the night,
Penguin
couldn't
sleep.

So Ellen had to bring him downstairs
and walk round and round with him,
patting his back.

The next morning everyone was tired.
Mum said, "What we need is a nice day
out. Where shall we go?" Ellen chose
the park with the farm animals.

Ellen and Penguin were so
excited they ran all the
way down the path to
where the animals lived.

They saw some lambs and
a family of little startled chicks.

Penguin's favourites were the
snuffly piglets with curly tails.

Ellen liked the baby rabbits,
snuggling together in the grass.

While Mum was unpacking the lunch,
the baby started crying again.
"Could you try and cheer him up?" said Mum.

Penguin wasn't sure what
to do, but Ellen said,
"Poor baby."

They tried a rattle
from his bag,

and a bear
and a book,
but he went
on crying.

Then Penguin did a little dance.

The baby stopped crying and looked.

Ellen and Penguin danced
round and round and got
more and more dizzy.

They collapsed in a
heap, laughing.

And the baby joined in.
"Our baby loves us," said Ellen.
And they both agreed that new baby
brothers weren't so bad after all.